CW00401592

A CRY FOR HELP

AMIE ROSEL

After going through a traumatic incident, Nina

moves to a new house in a new village to

recover and forget the events that landed her in

a coma. But as Nina starts to settle into her

new home she begins to experience strange

murmurings and whispers. Can it be her

imagination?

A result of the trauma caused by the incident?

or, is she going insane?

As Nina settles deeper into her new life, her

very sanity will be under question, but the end

result is more than she could ever imagine.

'Is all that we see or seem but a dream within a

dream?'

Edgar Allan Poe

I sit alone, huddled, in the corner. Afraid, so afraid. I feel like I am being shrouded with fear. An invisible bubble, surrounding me, holding me prisoner. The air has been drawn out of my lungs. I cannot draw a

breath. I am suffocating. Suddenly, a hand touches my

shoulder and I expel all the air I had been holding and

scream. A scream that came out - silent...

3 MONTHS AGO

'Good morning' my new neighbour shouted

across to me from the house opposite. I reply good

morning and continue carrying the last box of my

belongings out of my car into the house I had recently

purchased. I should have known new people moving

in would be a point of curiosity for people in the

neighbourhood. The woman comes across the street

and introduces herself as Jean. She appears quite

nondescript,#/ about five foot five with brown hair

which is tied back in a ponytail and wearing blue

denim jeans and a grey thin strap top, and open toe grey shoes. Not sure if this was the persona of an ordinary housewife, or if this was something I would have to get used to.

So this is how it's going to be, no peace and quiet. I welcome her albeit reluctantly, and inform her my name is Nina. We exchange pleasantries and as desperate as I am to get on, I can't just ignore her, so I bite the bullet and ask her if she would like a cup of tea or coffee. Of course she says yes, she wants to get into the house. I hunt for the kettle as I am still not sure where everything is. Mind you, being the sort of person I have become since the incident, I'm not certain of much anymore. Everything is labelled thank goodness and I find the kettle and a couple of mugs in the box marked 'kitchen stuff'.

I invite her into what is probably going to be 'the main living room'. It has a large bay window and looks out onto the straggled garden which is far enough away from the street to afford some privacy, which was one of the criteria I indicated when I was looking for a house. I had asked for a house that was semi-furnished and that is what I got. Kerb appeal was sufficient to draw the eye with lovely Blanco Grey slate porcelain tile paving leading up to a large cream stone facade tucked off the street behind an overgrown garden, a tiled roof which would probably need work soon, but it looked sturdy enough for now with lovely fronted bay windows. In the main living room, long velvet brown drapes hang at the windows with what was once probably a very nice cream net. It's quite a large room with resplendent sunlight penetrating through the shadows reflecting the light with dust motes dancing in tune to the branches swaying outside. Adjoining the main room is the dining room and kitchen. Walking into the dining room you are greeted by walls painted a bright sunlight yellow, with two french doors which are overlaid with plain cream curtains leading out onto the back garden. Outside there is a lovely view of the river which is situated at the end of pine decking enclosed in a wooden fence. On the decking are a couple of loungers and a metal bistro table with two matching chairs. The dining room also has access to the kitchen.

Going through the adjoining door, a big cream and black kitchen presented itself containing a large white marble covered central island with storage space that would be suitable for eating on until the dining room was furnished. Although it appeared somewhat dated, it was still nice enough. I have already got ideas of what I will be doing in the sitting room, shutters not net and possibly some voiles, although I am not sure what colour yet. I will wait to get a feel for the house before I decide. In the main living room, sparse furniture consists of two brown leather wing armchairs facing a whitewashed stone fireplace with a wide wooden mantlepiece and recesses on each side, possibly thinking about getting some bookshelves in there later. I am looking forward to lighting the fire when it gets cold. Rosewood flooring covered the floor with a Queen Anne coffee table placed between the two chairs which affords us some comfort as we settle down with our drinks.

Jean starts asking me personal questions, questions that I don't want to answer so I change the topic of conversation back to her, asking her how long she has lived here, what the neighbourhood is like and what entertainment there is available. Not that I intend to participate in any. Jean is quite chatty and before long I know she has lived here for eight years with her husband and two sons, both who are currently away in college. As we talk, I can sense her trying - not successfully - to hide the fact that she is taking in everything she can see, whether or not to pass the information onto her husband or other neighbours. It doesn't matter I suppose. I ask her about the previous tenants and I notice her eyes sparkle with enthusiasm as if she is about to impart some juicy piece of knowledge or perhaps local gossip.

'Well', she says. 'There's been a number of tenants since we moved in. No one seems to stay long though. I don't know why, it's such a nice place to live'. She says overly brightly. 'Of course, some parts of the house could do with a makeover as it's rather dated having been rented out before you bought it'. I inform her that is what I have in mind. She relaxes and seems pleased. 'Please let me know if you would like some help', she gushes. 'I'm a dab hand at painting. You must come over and join us for dinner. It would be nice for you to meet my husband'.

I told her I would be happy too some other time but that I had rather a lot to get through before I could think of food, especially as I wanted to sleep in my own bed tonight and needed to hunt out bedding and stuff.

'Well, if you won't come to us, I will bring something over. You can't possibly want to cook your first night here'.

I accepted that I was losing the battle and thanked her and said that would be nice. We said our goodbyes with the promise that she would see me later.

Seeing as I was going to have company tonight even though it was with reluctance, I thought I had better sort out somewhere for us to eat just in case they decided to stay. As if I didn't have enough to do! I started by moving our used cups out to the kitchen and decided that if we were going to have a meal it should be in the kitchen. I dug out cleaning materials and made a start on cleaning the cupboards and putting away all the dishes and utensils out of the box. I decided I needed to buy more as there were so many cupboards in the kitchen I needed to fill and a large black fridge freezer that looked a little sad with my meagre offerings in it at the moment. There was also a black range dual cooker that I looked forward to using. Long white marble countertops complemented a double stainless steel sink, microwave, dishwasher and washer completed the kitchen with Mexican tiles on the floor. Not too dated then. Happy with the work I had accomplished and deciding it was clean enough for company, I decided to sort out the bedroom in preparation for what I hoped would be a good night's sleep.

It was quite dark going up the stairs that curved at the bottom with the third step wider than the others at the curve. Grey fitted carpet lined the stairs and dark wood tongue and groove panelling covered the walls. Only a single light situated at the bottom and top of the stairs illuminated the way, I intended to change that as soon as possible. The stairs led up to a landing which consisted of five doors. On closer inspection three of the doors opened into the bedrooms, one was a bathroom and one was a linen closet, there was also a door that I assumed led to the attic as I had not yet explored that area. I couldn't wait to make the house mine, somewhere to relax and feel safe especially after the trauma I had endured. I pushed that thought to the back of my mind not wanting or needing to revisit that. I opened all the doors to look inside the rooms, all of which seemed to be a good size and could house a double bed comfortably. The decoration in the bedroom at the front seemed to indicate that it had belonged to a child, as the decor consisted of walls painted in blue with a fresco of horses adorning the walls. Flooring consisted of a lighter blue fitted carpet, lighter spaces on the floor highlighted where a bed and wardrobe must have once stood. The room seemed to be bathed in golden sunshine emanating from the windows that held a blue roman blind. I thought what a perfect room it was for a young child. The other front bedroom was quite nondescript and really needed some serious TLC as it looked like it had been abandoned, with no paper or paint on the walls, just a blank canvas ready for a work of art. The bedroom at the back seemed to be the most inviting, with double bay windows overlooking the garden and the pine decking leading down to the river. This too was surprisingly well furnished, decorated in pale peach with a small armoire, a double bed with a pine headboard and pine bedside tables on each side to match. Bronze lamps stood on each side table with the same colour shades. Frilled peach curtains covered the windows and also matched the bedspread which covered a brand new mattress still in its plastic protective covering. I have to admit, this kind of colour scheme was not to my taste and I decided to take the plunge and dig out my own bedding to put on the bed. Curtains could stay for now. I tried the lamps to make sure they were working and thankfully they were, not that I was scared of the dark but it's always nice to make sure these things are functional.

Having changed the bed and put out a few personal accessories, I was feeling rather grubby after the day's work. I decided it would be nice to have a shower and change before my visitors came. I dug out my toiletries, and with a large white fluffy towel and comfy slippers I went to have a shower. The bathroom was ideal with a huge walk-in shower, surrounded by white marble tiles and black glass panels. A beautiful white fitted bath with inlaid gold mixer taps, a white porcelain sink and matching toilet completed the look of a bathroom well designed for comfort. Considering the rest of the house was so drab, this was a pleasant surprise. I started running the shower to get the required temperature and began to undress in preparation for a luxurious shower. I placed my towel on the white porcelain sink which was conveniently situated next to the shower. I heard a noise and thought Jean had returned even though I was sure I had locked the doors. I opened the bathroom door to see who could be there, annoyed, as I was looking forward to a

hot shower with no interruptions, but of course there

was no-one there - it was just my imagination. I left

the door open just in case, not entirely sure why but

some instinct told me to. Wish I hadn't.

I stepped into the now steaming shower feeling

really pampered having a double walk-in power

shower all to myself. It was nothing like my last place

where you had to stand tailor straight just to feel the jet

of water over you, and don't blink, the water would

freeze, power shower, more like shower with no

power. The hot needles seemed to penetrate deep into

my skin and I felt my overstretched nerves relax. I

lathered my hair, washed out the shampoo and put a

conditioner on which I usually left on for one minute.

As I stood there luxuriating in the moment, the hot

needles on my skin, I sensed movement by the door. I could not see clearly as the black glass doors were steamed up. I turned my head but of course again my imagination was working overtime. There was no one there. I started to get an uneasy feeling and quickly washed the conditioner out of my hair and finished showering. I reached out for my towel that I had placed on the sink next to the shower and reached for thin air, it was not there, it was on the floor. I assumed I had not put it on the sink unit securely. Still, I had the feeling someone was looking at me. I looked at the bathroom door once again and, for a spark of a moment, I thought I saw someone looking around the door. As the landing was quite dark and the bathroom steamed up, I couldn't be sure. I didn't scream as I consider myself to be quite a rational person however I was annoyed to think that someone had gotten into the house. I quickly picked up my towel and wrapped it around my still wet body, not waiting to dry myself off. I went out to the landing convinced I would find someone there. There was no one there except whispering shadows, always whispering. Putting it down to a new house and exhaustion I promptly forgot what I thought I had seen and heard, got dressed in jeans and a T-shirt, and went downstairs to make sure I had some wine to put in the fridge.

Despite my misgivings, it turned out to be a pleasant evening. Jean and her husband who she introduced as Paul, was six foot plus, dark wavy hair and cleanly shaven, both came over with a lovely salad and pizza. Perfect for a first night meal I thought. I opened the bottle of wine for Jean and me as Paul said he preferred a beer which he had brought with them, and we settled down to enjoy the evening. They were surprisingly good company, discussing their boys and how well they were doing in college, one hoping to be a doctor, the other undecided, hedging his bets between being a solicitor or a teacher. Jean and Paul agreed they would be happy to support them in whichever career either of them choose. But you could see the pride in them both as they talked about their sons. I wondered if I would ever have the opportunity to meet someone and share the easy camaraderie they seemed to have. I started yawning which was very rude of me but Jean said that they should go and I should get to bed after a hard day moving in. There was no argument from me. We said our goodnights with a promise to repeat the evening. I decided the dishes and glasses could wait until the morning and made my way to bed turning out all the lights on my way. I had just started up the stairs and placed my foot on the third step when suddenly, it felt like something was rushing past me. A cold shiver went through me but I thought I must have had too much wine. I had a wash, cleaned my teeth, undressed and got into bed which now had my own white 500 thread egyptian cotton bedding on it. I snuggled down into the goose down duvet and realised how exhausted I felt and was hoping I would be able to get straight off to sleep. I must have dozed off because sometime later I woke up feeling cold, as if the blankets had been pulled off me but I was still tucked up warm. I had the slight sensation that someone was whispering to me again; but I have to admit, after my 'accident', I was still frequently hearing whispers. The clinical psychologist I had been previously seeing had said that I might have recurring visions of what happened that night. That is why I wanted to move somewhere where it was quiet and I could recover from the 'incident', as I had come to think of it.

CHAPTER 2

I woke up quite refreshed despite having interrupted sleep. I washed and dressed in khaki crop trousers and a beige t-shirt with sandals to match and made my way downstairs for the first breakfast in my new home and made plans for what I was going to do that day. I wanted to replace the lights on the stairs and start looking at new furniture. I decided it would be nice to see what they had on offer in the village and wondered if Jean would like to accompany me and show me around. It would be a good opportunity to get to know each other better. I finished breakfast which to be honest was just toast, jam and cup of tea. I washed all the dishes from breakfast and last night leaving the intricate workings of the dishwasher for another time. I thought I would wander the rooms to get a feel for what I might need. The fireplace in the room I had designated as a sitting room needed something ornamental above it I thought. I decided a mirror would look nice above and I knew just the one I would like. I wondered if they had anything like it in the village. The sun was shining outside in a beautiful azure sky, slow moving wisps of clouds trailed across the sky with sunbeams dancing in and out of the trees with the birds in full chorus. It looked like it was going to be a beautiful day so I decided everything else could wait.

I grabbed my purse and my keys and went out into the sunshine. Jean was outside emptying bins and she waved when she saw me. I made my way across to her and asked her if she would like to come shopping with me. She seemed pleased at this simple request and said yes, it would be a nice time to get to know each other better. It took Jean all of ten minutes to go into the house and change into clothing similar to what I was wearing: jeans, sandals and a summer top. We jumped into my silver Nissan Micra and away we went.

As it turned out, Jean was able to take me to a second hand shop just at the end of the village which was surprisingly large: large enough to be a town with a variety of different shops accommodating choices for everyone. It was fun to look at the various items on offer and, while I never expected to find what I was looking for in this village shop, but by some stroke of luck, I managed to find the exact mirror I had thought would look good above the fireplace, and even two chandelier shades for the lights on my stairs. Feeling happy with my purchases, and to show Jean how much I appreciated her coming with me, I invited her for lunch at the pub in the village. The pub was a quaint little place that appeared to be a former cottage that had been refurbished. On closer scrutiny, I could see I was wrong, it was two former cottages joined together. Regardless of what it had been, it served meals and that's all we wanted. As we walked in I took in the decor and ambience of the pub and found it to be very soothing. There was lovely old stone everywhere and a wood burning fireplace cast in the same stone as the walls throughout. The pub was compartmentalised, old fashioned these days in the time of gastro pubs, but in keeping with the area. The pub consisted of a lounge, a bar and a restaurant. We could hear muted voices coming from the bar as we looked in and saw a couple of gentleman cradling pints. In the far corner stood a snooker table and a jukebox. Not wanting to disturb them, we asked the barman behind the bar if they served food in the lounge and he said yes.

We entered the lounge which was surprisingly empty at this time of day as it was lunchtime and sat next to the stone fireplace, although the fire was not lit at this moment one could imagine the cosiness of the place once it was lit and the ambience an open fire would create. Dark wood tables with velvet backed chairs made the whole room seem warm. We perused the menu and then ordered lunch at the bar which consisted of salad and quiche for us both. Jean had a glass of chardonnay while I stuck to a fizzy drink because I was driving. I thought I would find out more about the place I was going to call home and I asked Jean to tell me a little bit about the village and she appeared pleased that I valued her opinion.

She told me the village started life as a small hamlet that got so popular with people it just kept growing. It now had a population of 2,500 inhabitants and was mostly crime free. As she said this I had a sneaky suspicion she was omitting something important but she continued to explain that as the village was situated away from all the noise and pollution that big cities have and if I wanted to go for a walk, there was a diversity of crops and flowers to see as well as more than a few well established trees. She also explained that the local bus service was ideal for getting into town where the transport was varied and easily accessible with trains travelling to a variety of destinations. Feeling as if I had gotten enough information for that day we left for home. I dropped Jean off at her house with promises to get together soon and parked in front of mine, exhausted, but pleased with my purchases.

CHAPTER 3

The next couple of weeks were quite busy as I started to decorate the house to what I wanted. I donated the old furniture to the second hand shop I had purchased the mirror from, they seemed quite pleased to take them off my hands. Up above the fireplace went the mirror and I was quite pleased with myself that I had managed to put it up without incident. Next on the list was the lights on the stairs. One hour later everything had been done. New chandeliers made such a difference, even seeming to make the panelling lighter. In the sitting room I painted the walls a lovely antique cream, with two matching cream leather sofas facing each other with a purple throw and scatter cushions. I placed the sofa's each side of the fireplace so that when it was lit it would be cosy. A glass coffee table sat in between the two sofas to complement and finish the look I was aiming for. New cream drapes with bishop sleeves and purple contrasting voiles adorned the windows. Satisfied with my work that day, I decided to have a shower and relax with some wine. I went into the kitchen to fetch myself a glass of white wine, I had both a chardonnay and sauvignon blanc to choose from. While debating which one to have I heard an almighty crash come from the sitting room. I immediately forgot the wine and rushed back into the sitting room expecting to find glass everywhere but, there, on the floor, was the mirror. What was strange and to me, very unusual, was the mirror was whole. Not a scratch or a crack. Absolutely nothing. It just sat on the floor, completely missing the mantelpiece and just sitting there as if I had just placed it there. Not a scratch on the wall where I had hung it. Nail was still in place just as it was when I hammered it in. I was so relieved there was no damage, I just assumed I had not hung it properly and put it back on the wall. Feeling shook up and deciding to leave the wine till later, I thought I would try my luck instead and look in the attic space. Who knows I could use it for a spare room or study if it was big enough.

I climbed up the stairs, now with the new lights which made such a difference to the ambience of the stairs. As I reached the top of the stairs I looked around for something to open the attic door with. Thank goodness, placed in the shadows next to the bathroom door, there was a pole with a hook on the end to pull down the attic door. I inserted the hook into the catch on the attic door and was pleasantly surprised that there was also a ladder that automatically descended when the door was opened. I ascended the ladder and looked around for a light switch hoping I wouldn't have to go looking for a torch. I found one just within reach of the attic door and breathed a sigh of relief I wouldn't have to go searching.

The attic was quite large and airy which would suit whatever I decided to go with. The only thing I wasn't fussy on was the continuation of the tongue and groove panelling on the walls. There were, however, two skylights in the roof which were letting some lovely rays of sunshine through, highlighting the many dust motes dancing in the floor. Flooring had already been installed thankfully which would save me that job! A few boxes were in the room and what I assumed was a child's forgotten drum kit and a small rocking chair tossed into the corner, otherwise it was empty. I decided that this would make a lovely study and was planning what I could comfortably get up through the attic door. A bit ambitious I know but, well why not. I sat down on the bare wooden floor while contemplating all of this, and just for a moment, in the still silence, I thought I heard a child crying. Hairs stood up on my arms as if a cold wind had passed over me. I listened more intently but heard nothing. Deciding it must have come from outside, I got up to go back downstairs. As I did, something cold brushed right through me. When I say right through me, that is exactly what it felt like; as if a spirit had walked into my skin and walked through me to get back out, a bit fancy I know but that's how I felt. I looked up to make sure the skylights weren't open thinking that the cold must have come from there but they were shut. Oh well, I thought, the house seems to be making me fanciful. I gave myself a shake and went back down the ladders and shut the attic door with the pole provided, I had my delayed glass of wine, which turned into a bottle!

CHAPTER 4

I was certainly getting a feel for the house or should I say, it was getting a feel for me. Going into the passage that led to the stairs, I picked up my feet to step over what was on the floor. I looked down to see what I had left there so I could move it before going up the stairs and I realised there was nothing there. I continued my way up the stairs and once again, on the third step, it felt like a breath of wind brush past me. I decided that there must be an opening somewhere where a draught must be getting through. Darkness fell, and I started to get ready for bed. I turned the sheets down and decided to have a hot shower before retiring. Steam was coming from the shower as I stepped in, like spectral wisps of fine gossamer, floating in the ethereal space occupying the ceiling. I felt like I was lost in this sublime moment of time and did not want it to end. Coming out of my self hypnosis, I realised that I had been in the shower longer than I had intended. I reached for my towel, once again on the floor, and was about to step out, when I sensed someone there. I turned the shower off and pulled the towel into the cubicle. Shivering, not with cold, but apprehension. I stepped out of the shower, towel now wrapped around me, and peered through the steam to open the window to let it out. I

opened the window and tried to peer through the steam
to see who was there.

'Who's there?' I asked. No reply.

The silence seemed to be whispering all around me.
A cold sweat broke out all over me, reversing the
effects of the hot shower. The steam cleared and I
braved the eerie silence to see what was there. I put
my head slowly around the bathroom door, afraid in
case there was someone there about to chop my head
off! We've all seen Freddie right!. My senses were so
overstrung I could have snapped at the slightest sound.
I stepped out of the bathroom ready to face whoever
was out there, and I faced emptiness. There was no-
one there.

Shaking, I went to bed. Curling up under the
duvet I assumed a foetal position, wrapping my arms

tightly around me to keep myself safe, still shaking,

wondering if the 'incident' was responsible for

everything I imagined was happening to me. I decided

I needed to talk to someone about what was happening

in my life and realised I needed to talk to a

professional. Making this decision I settled down to

rest. I didn't think I would sleep but exhaustion took

over and I must have dozed off. I awoke at stupid am

and felt the cold shrouding me. Puffs of little white

clouds emanated from my mouth as I pulled the

blankets up around me hoping to get warm, but there

seemed to be a struggle. The blankets seemed to pull

against me in the opposite direction. It felt like

someone was deliberately holding them and tugging

them away from me. I tell you, the way my nerves

were, I started imagining all sorts. The rational part of

me decided that I must have tucked them in too tight when I made the bed, the irrational part of me was afraid to think at all. With trembling hands, I managed to reach the lamp to put on the light - how brave was that! I needed to get an Alexa so I could just turn the lamp on with my voice.

The lamp shone a pale yellow but at least it chased some of the shadows away. I peered at the bottom of the bed expecting to see someone there, but again, nothing and no-one. By now I was so uptight there was no way I would be able to get back to sleep. I thought a warm drink might help me relax, so I got out of bed, slipped my slippers on and a dressing gown and went onto the landing to go downstairs. Usually, I am not bothered about putting lights on, but tonight, I felt like I needed as much illumination as possible.

Before my hand could touch the light switch, I felt it;
A coldness so numbing, I felt for a moment as if I was
encased in ice. Deep down, in the very depths of my
being, it felt as if my very soul was in pain, slowly
dying, withering, crying out. I just stood there
desperately trying to hold on to it to make sense of it.
Of why it was happening to me. Dark silhouetted
shadows walked past me, around me, through me and
disappeared into nothingness. I released the breath I
didn't realise I had been holding.

I forced myself out of that surreal moment,
with what inner strength I really couldn't say. I
managed to reach out my hand and flick on the light
switch and suddenly, I was bathed in the warm glow of
the chandelier. Everything was as it should be and I
started to breathe again thinking in my tired and

wound up state, I must have imagined it all. The thought of a warm drink still held its appeal, and I continued downstairs. I had nearly got to the bottom of the stairs when, on the third step, I felt a small hand grab me. I was so surprised that I floundered and fell down the remaining steps. I must have hit my head on the facing wall because all I remember is waking up some time later, cold, and with a pounding headache. Although it was late, I felt I did not want to stay in the house any longer that night. I phoned Jean and it wasn't long before she picked up the phone; as if she had been waiting for the call. I told her that I had fallen down the stairs and needed some help. I didn't elaborate as I wasn't sure myself what had happened or how to explain it to her. She came straight over and looked at where I had hit my head. She said there didn't seem to be too much damage but thought it would be a good idea for me to stay with her that night so she could keep an eye on me in case of concussion. I gathered a few things and willingly went with her. Jean showed me where her spare room was and I was happy to settle into the bed.

I slept late the next morning waking with a slight headache. I felt guilty because I was in someone else's house. I washed and dressed in the en-suite bathroom looking in the mirror to see what damage I had inflicted on myself. A slight bruise was beginning to show on my forehead and I knew I was lucky I didn't have a black eye. I made my way downstairs ready to make my apologies. The stairs came down to a landing very similar in design to mine, so, thinking I knew the way, I turned towards the kitchen. There was no one around and all I could hear were voices carrying through from outside. I followed the voices into the garden and discovered Jean and Paul talking in hushed tones with very concentrated looks on their faces. I heard Jean say to Paul, "What do you think? Do you think she knows anything? What if she finds out the truth?

"We must just continue watching her and if she does discover anything, we do what we always do, we deal with it". Paul said. Jean spotted me and, immediately, her face and voice changed to one of concern.

"Nina", she gushed, "how are you feeling?"

Apart from a slight headache and severe embarrassment, I told her I was fine. She clucked like a mother hen with a chick and said I must have some breakfast to help me feel better. I felt like I could only manage tea and toast even though Jean wanted me to have a full cooked breakfast. I declined and said tea and toast was fine but

thanked her for the offer apologising if I had hurt her feelings. The ever generous hostess, Jean said she was happy to accommodate whatever I felt I could eat. After breakfast and numerous questions from Jean making sure I was ok. I felt that it was time to go home. I thanked her and we hugged and she said as long as I felt I was feeling better, and to promise if I needed anything I would call, she was happy to see me leave waving goodbye as she turned to go into her own home.

CHAPTER 5

As soon as I got home, I checked the stairs to convince myself that I had imagined it all. As I expected there was nothing there to indicate why I had fallen. I phoned my sister, Katie, to tell her what had happened to me and she said she would be down the next day.

True to her word she arrived on my doorstep with the two boys in tow. Rowdy and already bored from the journey, they asked if they could explore the house and I gave them permission to do so. They went off with a whoop and a holler and my sister and I went into the kitchen and sat at the centre island where I made us a cup of tea. We could hear the boys upstairs

opening and closing doors, they came streaming down
the stairs and asked if they could go up and explore the
attic. I told them there was a set of drums up there
they could have a go on if they were good. They
promised they would be so I went up the stairs with
them and opened the attic door for them telling them
to be careful. I went back down to Katie who was still
in the kitchen and she asked me to tell her what had
happened. I explained as best I could, not being able
to remember everything. She sympathised with the
bruise on my head and we joked how I seemed to have
a hard head.

It was getting close to dinner time and we
hadn't heard from the boys for a while due to the
distance and soundproofing in the attic. My sister
went to call them down and see what they wanted for

lunch. They came down and asked if they could go back up to play with the little boy. I asked them what little boy and they said the one in the attic who the drums belonged to. I asked them how they knew that and they said the little boy had told them. I looked at my sister and she looked at me as if to say 'what boy?' I told them that there was no little boy up there, only them two. Thinking they were trying to pull a fast one, I asked them to show me.

Katie and I followed the boys up to the attic and I could see the apprehension on my sister's face which must have been mirrored on mine. I reassured her there couldn't possibly be anyone up there and they must be having us going. We climbed into the attic and I asked the boys where the other boy was. They looked around and said that he must have gone home for his lunch as they could no longer see him. I looked at my sister and saw the relief on her face which must have been reflected on mine. She gave the boys a row for making up stories even though they insisted they hadn't, but they knew better than to argue with their mother. After lunch, which consisted of pasta and a salad, we went out to the back garden to sit on the decking and let the boys do some fishing with a pole and some string I had managed to find in one of the kitchen drawers. I didn't know if there were any fish in the water but it kept them quiet while we caught up on the gossip.

We relaxed in the sun and she asked me what was going on. I tried to explain to her about the things that had been happening to me like, the whispers and the silences and the strange feeling of being watched, but I couldn't convey to her in words the dread and the helplessness I had felt, the feeling of out of control, of how the shadows seemed to be oppressing me and how I felt like I was walking through thick fog whose tendrils were trying to keep me from moving. I tried to explain the events of the past month but she laughed and said I was getting really fanciful and that perhaps I had banged my head harder than the doctors had thought in the hospital. She suggested it might be a good idea to see a neurologist just in case, especially with the secondary bang on my head which may have aggravated the original injury.

CHAPTER 6

It was just a random attack, totally

unprovoked. No sense to it really. I was leaving the

theatre with my sister who for once, had managed to

find a babysitter for her twin boys. We were discussing

the play, walking down towards the train station which

meant walking down a ramp to get to the station

platform, illuminated only by one solitary lamp. We

were on our own on the way down the ramp when we

heard whispering behind us. We both turned

expecting to see more theatre goers behind us hoping

to catch the same train, and noticed that we were

being followed by two men who looked like shadows in

the night as the light was behind them and we were

unable to make out their features. I asked them if they

wanted to pass us as we were going slow but they said

no they wanted something off us. They drew closer to

us and I asked them what they wanted, they smirked and the look in their eyes suggested they wanted something we were not prepared to give. I told my sister to run down the ramp and as I faced them one of them went to run after her. I stuck my foot out and he fell forward with a howl as he landed on his face. The other one grabbed hold of me and I tried to defend myself by trying to kick him in the balls but I got punched in the face for my troubles which totally disoriented me as I felt the pain cascading through me and the coppery taste of blood filled my mouth.

The other one got up and grabbed my bag and started searching through it. I only had a few pounds left after the theatre and would have willingly given it to them to go away but they seemed intent on finding something. In the midst of my pain, I thought I heard sirens and hoped that my sister had managed to get help. The two men must have also realised that there was help coming for me and afraid of getting caught, the one holding me gave me another punch and threw me against the wall, hard. I remember knocking my head on the wall and the excruciating pain that went through me like rippling water, I blissfully faded into oblivion. The next thing I remember was three days later waking up in hospital with my sister beside me, pale. I asked her what had happened. She asked me what I remembered and all I could say was 'whispering' behind me. She told me that I had had a nasty knock to the head besides bruising to my face where I had been hit. Apparently, I had been in an induced coma for three days.

CHAPTER 7

We sat there in the warm sunshine enjoying the peace and quiet when the peace was disturbed by the boys arguing. They were both sitting on the edge of the deck with their feet dangling in the water while they tried to catch 'fish'. They seemed to be talking to someone in between them when Robert suddenly fell into the shimmering water, although the sun was shining, it must have been cold. My sister ran to the edge of the deck and grabbed Robert's hand and pulled him to safety. She asked them both what had happened although it seemed obvious Robert had lost his balance.

'He pushed me in', Robert said.

She turned to Richard and asked him why he had pushed his brother in and he said it wasn't him it was Marc.

'Who on earth is Marc?' she said.

'You know, the little boy from upstairs', Robert said.

'He said I wasn't playing his drums properly and I said I was. He said they were his drums and I shouldn't touch them. I told him aunty Nina said it was ok for us to use them, and he said it wasn't her house, she didn't give the orders, it was his house and then he pushed me in'. My sister went as pale as she had been that first day I had seen her in the hospital. 'There is no little boy' she said. 'You must stop making up stories'.

'But Mam, we were playing with him, he was sitting by us fishing, didn't you see him? Richard said'.

Katie and the boys left soon after. I think Katie was too shaken up to stay with me much longer even though I was hoping she would have stayed. The boys wanted to stay and play with Marc again even though we explained there was no Marc. However, they insisted and that was when Katie decided it was time to leave. I attempted to reassure her that the boy's imagination was working overtime even though I was aware of my own thoughts and feelings regarding strange happenings that could not be explained. I decided that it was about time I went to see a specialist and find out what really was happening to me.

CHAPTER 8

As I went to bed that night, I was still a little shaken by what the boys had said they had seen. I was getting really fanciful as I even checked the bedding wasn't tucked in too tight before getting into bed. Sleep seemed a lifetime away so I turned the bedside lamp on to illuminate the darkness as I lay there with a myriad of thoughts penetrating my brain. Suddenly, there was a flash of lightning and I could hear the rain pelting down outside. Just about right I thought; a storm to match my mood. I lay there for a while just listening to the storm and watching the quick strobe of lightning as it flashed through the windows. I had left the curtains open and the window just a little as it had been warm and muggy before bed. Now I knew why.

The thunder seemed to be hovering above the house getting more and more intense with each peal. The onslaught of lightning was never ending, quick, strobing lights filled the whole room, I'm sure the whole house. The lamp I had left on seemed to take on a life of its own, dimming, lighting, dimming again. I turned it off just in case it decided to blow up on me. The extended barrage of lightning continued highlighting the shimmering shadows in the room, seeming intent on playing tricks with my eyes. A total obliteration of the normal senses continued with the smell of ozone penetrating the air through the open window. Dark silhouettes continued to bounce and undulate in mid air like the haunting of spirits let out on halloween.

What occurred next was straight out of a horror film.

The shadows became more menacing as the lightning began to disperse. Previous dark shadows became phantasmagoric images displaying optical illusions all around me. Images began to morph in front of me. Pale insubstantial, wraithlike figures appeared, no shape or substance attached itself. They seemed to coagulate in a circle and perform some macabre dance like some old fashioned polka. Fear claimed me, I wanted to scream but I couldn't make a sound, my vocal cords were struck dumb, I couldn't even make a whisper. Out of this unearthly sight, a small figure appeared and approached me.

'Help me', it said.

I fainted.

CHAPTER 9

I awoke and I sat in the oppressive silence which seemed strange after the thunder and lightning. Whispering came again, but from where? I sat motionless, so still, waiting.

"Where are you?' I asked.

"I'm here", a small voice responded, "please find me".

I screamed, "where are you?"

The silence received me. Was I imagining all of this, were my delusions real or a figment of my imagination! Was the bang on my head far more traumatic than I realised? All I can hear is whispers, whispers encompassing me in the silence. It was as if I was back in that hell place where I had been attacked, it was just one extensive unremitting nightmare as if reality and dreams had contrived to traverse time. I felt so helpless, so vulnerable to what was happening to me but unable to comprehend the extent of it all. Events of the past weeks unfolded before my eyes in a surreal cycle, in a strange illusive sequence.

The next day, I rang Dr Bateman who had been my primary care specialist when I came out of the coma. I spoke to his secretary and explained what was happening to me and told her I needed Dr Bateman's help. She told me I was very lucky as there had been a cancellation for the next day and asked me if I would like to go in then? I jumped at the suggestion and considered myself lucky indeed.

Nothing eventful happened during the night and I was able to get up semi-refreshed and prepare for my appointment with Dr Bateman. After a shower and some breakfast, I left the house to go to the doctor's office but, as soon as I went outside I spotted Jean. I'm sure she's watching my house. I didn't have the time or the inclination to speak to her so I gave her a wave and jumped into my car before she could engage me in conversation. Arriving at Dr Bateman's building I wasn't sure how I felt. I wanted to turn around and leave but knew I needed an explanation to what was going on in my life, or rather what I thought was happening to me.

Dr Bateman's office looked more like a plush apartment than a doctor's surgery. Plush beige carpet with wine coloured Chesterfield chairs, muted hessian paint on the walls and some prints I could swear were originals. I introduced myself to Dr Bateman's secretary who looked like she had just stepped out of a magazine with blonde hair tied up in a topknot and wearing a suit that looked very expensive. She asked me to take a seat. It was no hardship; everything was geared towards the patient's comfort from the seating offered in the form of a two seater settee to the plush Chesterfield chairs and the coffee machine and water cooler situated in the corner.

I was waiting for about five minutes when Dr Bateman himself opened his door and invited me into his office. Dr Bateman was the personification of a successful doctor. Although only five foot eleven, he exuded health and wealth. Strong looking handsome man with a mane of blond hair on his head, not a strand out of place, clean shaven. Looked more like a film star than a doctor. On entering, I noticed that the colour scheme had been followed through in here and felt like I was in a time warp, slightly disoriented as it seemed I had just taken a step forward, not into another room but a duplicate of the one I had left.

"Now then Nina', he said, 'what's this I hear about you hearing voices?'

I started trembling and he asked me if I would like a glass of water, I said 'yes please', and as he went to get me one, I took the moment to compose myself and not turn into a blubbering idiot.

'Now, tell me what's happened'.

I tried to explain myself as best I could, leaving nothing out, not the whispering, not the feeling of someone watching me or of the feeling of being grabbed in the darkness, the shadows that seemed to be in disguise and were really spirits out to get me. All that time Dr Bateman just sat there and listened, not murmuring or making a sound. After I felt that I had worn myself out with talking, Dr Bateman went, 'ahh right'. Let's talk about what happened to you first and perhaps this will help you understand what you feel like you could be going through'.

'When a person suffers an injury to the brain such as you did, certain chemical processes that govern the brain can be altered. Any head trauma can cause swelling of the brain and, because it is such a small space, it can grow in volume, the fluid in the brain will then push it up. The possible outcome of this is that as a result of this event, the swelling can push down on the brain stem. This can result in damage to the RAS (Reticular Activating System). This is the area of the brain responsible for arousal and awareness'. He continued, 'by putting you into a drug induced coma and lowering your body temperature, we were able to allow your brain to rest and recover. The idea is to lessen the amount of energy required by different areas of the brain. This then allows the brain to heal as the swelling goes down and those areas are protected'. 'Is any of this making any sense to you?' he asked me.

'So', I said, ' what you are trying to tell me is that what I am hearing and seeing is a result of my head trauma?'

'possible side effects of putting you into a drug induced coma can lead to some patients experiencing nightmares and hallucinations, they can be extremely intense to the auditory senses', he said.

'Any one who has gone through a traumatic injury to the brain such as yours can expect the auditory process and/or sensorineural hearing to be affected. Individuals can develop a range of impairments including, cognitive impairment, language, although I have not seen any evidence of that in you. Also psychological and sensory deficits, all or some of these can have an adverse effect on a person. Such as when we use auditory processing, because of your head injury, it could cause you to hear voices. Don't worry you are not experiencing schizophrenic hallucinations', he laughed. 'If you start hearing voices following a traumatic experience, this can be construed as a psychological process that the brain has created to handle any stress. I understand that you have recently moved? Are you aware that moving is considered to be one of the biggest stress factors next to divorce and death especially as you did it so soon after what you experienced?'.

I sat there still afraid to breathe. 'So all this is normal?' I asked.

'Normal for someone who has experienced a head trauma', he said. ' I am inclined to think now after hearing everything you believe you have experienced that you could be suffering from post traumatic stress disorder. Do you know anything about PTSD?'

'I've heard of it' I said, 'but no, I don't know much about it'.

'Well', he said, 'let me tell you a little about it'.

PTSD is considered to be a condition caused by witnessing or experiencing a terrifying incident such as your attack. It can cause severe anxiety in a person which in turn, can change a person's physical and emotional reactions. Symptoms vary from person to person but specifically when a person is stressed, they can become easily frightened; especially when they have gone through a traumatic experience such as actual or threatened death. No-one is sure why PTSD happens but one thing is for sure, as with most mental health problems, real or imagined, PTSD can be triggered by a lot of things, for example, stress and going through a traumatic assault such as you endured.

I could carry out a psychological evaluation and prescribe some medication for you - some antidepressants can help with erratic sleep patterns known as SSRI, selective serotonin reuptake inhibitors, or even prazosin. These will help you to cope'.

'I don't want to start depending on drugs to get through each day', I said.

'Well, how about practising some coping strategies? For example, follow a healthy diet, get more rest and avoid caffeine. You need to break the cycle - if you start to feel anxious go for a walk, stay connected with people. Spend time with people who can support you whether it's family or friends. The choice is yours, but

I would like you to think about what I have said even if you are not happy with medication, seriously think about the coping strategies I have mentioned'.

I thanked Dr Bateman for his time and advice, promising to call if I needed to or if I changed my mind about the medication. I went away with my head full of information and tried to digest all the information he had given me. Was I really suffering with PTSD? It is possible I suppose based on what he said about it developing after a traumatic incident.

CHAPTER 10

As soon as I reached home I phoned Katie to pass on what the doctor had told me. 'I'm not surprised', she said. 'Something has had to give, you're holding everything in when you should be talking to someone'.

'I know', I told her, 'but it's not always easy if you think you're losing your mind'. She laughed and told me at least it was a start. Promising to come down on the weekend with the twins she said she had to go but would see me then.

The weekend arrived and as promised Katie arrived with the boys who once again wanted to go up the attic and play with the drums. I said ok as long as there were no more stories. They promised and off they went while Katie and I sat in the kitchen again with a cup of tea. Katie wanted all the details from the doctors and I was telling her when Richard came screaming down the stairs closely followed by Robert. Motherly instinct immediately took over and Katie rushed to the boys. They were both sobbing and it took five minutes before Katie could get them to tell us what was wrong. Both of them tried to explain in between their sobs so Katie took control and asked Richard to tell her what was wrong.

'It was that boy', he sobbed,

'we were playing with the drums and he said we couldn't after the last time, but you said he wasn't real so we ignored him but he just took the drum sticks off us and kept playing the drums and he wouldn't stop and then he just disappeared'.

Robert took over the story, 'he disappeared but the drums kept drumming they wouldn't stop, we asked them to but they just kept on going and going!. Mammy they really scared us'.

On hearing this I raced up the stairs to the attic but all was quiet, no little boy and no drums drumming. I did however get a sense of unease as it felt really cold and unwelcoming. I went back downstairs and told the boys to come back up the attic with me so they could see there was no-one there. 'No', they screamed, 'I want to go home'.

I looked at Katie and she had that concerned look on her face again.

'I know', I said, 'because you have had such a fright, let's all go out for lunch'. This seemed to appease the boys slightly and they agreed. Katie packed the boys' stuff together as fast as she could and I said we could go to the pub in the village. She loaded her belongings in her car while I went to get in mine. She caught my arm and said I needed to do something about the house. I could feel eyes on me and when I turned, Jean was watching intently. I waved to show her that I could see her and she waved back but looked a little embarrassed that I had caught her watching us.

We went to the local pub where the boys seemed to have got over their fright and Katie and I started discussing what I should do about the house as there was obviously something wrong there. I promised her that I would deal with it and we finished lunch. I asked her when I would see her again and she just said to wait until I knew what was going on with my house.

Reaching home, I decided it was about time I did try to find out what was happening in my house as I thought this was going to be my forever home. Whatever it was, if the boys were to be believed, it was manifesting itself in the attic. I made my way up to the attic and half expected something on the stairs to stop me going up there. The attic was the same as it had been when I left it before lunch. Quiet - no sound seemed to penetrate through the heavy panelling. I listened intently for any of the whispering I had heard before but was met only with heavy silence. I called out, 'hello', thinking I must be going crazy if I had to resort to talking to thin air! Of course there was no answer but I was determined I was going to find out what was going on. I went downstairs and picked up an old tape recorder I had acquired a long time ago. I set it to record and went back upstairs to place it in the attic, curious to see what would happen. I sat on the floor placing the tape recorder next to me and thought 'what a waste of bloody time', still, what did I have to lose. I sat there like an idiot listening for any sound that would penetrate the silence. It started to get late and I thought, 'what a bloody fool', I thought I might

as well call it a night when I heard hushed whispers.

Real or imagined?

'Help me', 'help me', a small tiny voice came from

nowhere and yet seemed to be everywhere.

 'Where are you?' I ask.

 'I'm here please find me', it whispered and faded

away.

PTSD my arse this is real! I feel so frustrated. If this

isn't my imagination what do I need to do? I grabbed

the tape recorder eager to hear what was on there, so I

knew I wasn't going mad and could decide what I

needed to do next.

I went into the sitting room and made myself

comfortable on one of the cream sofas, placed the tape

recorder on the glass table and pressed play. No sound

came from there except my breathing, but then it had

taken a while for the whisper to start. I sat there for

twenty minutes without a sound. 'Perhaps I had timed

it wrong', I thought and fast forwarded it, but again

nothing. I was getting really frustrated with myself

and fast-forwarded it again, but the only voice I heard

was my own, asking 'where are you?' 'God was I

really going mad?' Doubt crept into my mind and I

wondered if through my loneliness and frustrated

curiosity I would end up emotionally or even

physically in oblivion. Were the voices the onset of a

psychotic break, was what I thought I heard part of

delusional thoughts and beliefs was I experiencing

some form of paranoia through auditory

hallucinations? Or, was I being haunted? There was

only one way to find out and I was damned if I was going to let anyone tell me any different!

Chapter 11

The next day, I decided to do some research on what could be happening in my home. Not wanting Jean to know what I was doing, I went into the neighbouring town to the library. The library had been converted from an old grade 11 listed baptist chapel. Many of the original characteristics were still visible. Organ pipes rose high up into the ceiling now enclosed behind a glass window. No pews stood waiting for parishioners, in their place, rows and rows of books. Computers stood like robots along the one wall with sporadic seating placed around inviting people to sit in relative peace and quiet to read for a while or even take advantage of the free daily newspapers on display. It looked like the original balcony of polished wood was still in place behind which stood more rows of books. All choices catered for. I hope they had what I was looking for. I didn't want anyone to know what I was looking for, hell I wasn't even sure I knew what I was looking for! Witchcraft, hauntings, troubled spirits? Where to start? I decided the most sensible course would be to look through the different categories and see if anything resonated in my brain.

I found information on using a ouija board first and thought I might as well start with that as anything else. I know that many thought a ouija board was some kind of silly toy or gimmick but I thought I would check it out. I found information on using a Ouija Board by a ghost researcher called 'Dale Kaczmarek' who was a member of the 'Ghost

Research Society'. He stated that when spirits are contacted through a ouija board they are most often those who reside on 'the lower astral plane,' and the conditions when using a ouija board could be potentially dangerous and threatening to whoever would be using the board. Oh well, that was something to be aware of then. Kaczmarek was not alone in providing a warning. Other spiritualists stated that a ouija board was to be used at one's own discretion and they claimed that spirit boards and other means of connecting with the dead could be highly dangerous, acting as a possible gateway opening that would allow ghosts or other intangible entities to pass through into the users body. Some things that come through are dangerous and difficult to return.

I looked at each on its own merits and realised before I made a decision I first needed to establish if there was any real evidence of ghostly activity in my house. Did I have anything bizarre happening around me? I thought I did, thinking I was seeing something out of the corner of my eye in the bathroom, the towel dropping on the floor, not to mention the mirror falling off the wall. And the whispers - always whispers. I swear they are real. I'm not fooling myself into thinking that everything I was hearing or experiencing is a haunting. I'm well aware that some noises have a very easy explanation, such as the house settling down in the night, floors creaking settling down, drafts from open windows or poor ventilation, or - and the big one, my imagination.

Of course I have to ask myself if ghosts are real or not. I know there is no scientific perspective that supports the theory that ghosts are real, but I needed to find out if I am going mad or not. In my reading, I read that relationships with ghosts may be unusual but surely not impossible if there were so many accounts. I was not going to share this information with anyone, I didn't want anyone but me worrying about my mental health! I am aware ghosts only manifest themselves as residual energy and don't have thought processes or desires as we know them.

On returning home, I phoned my sister and told her what I had thought about doing. I expected her to be really sceptical and laugh at me saying I was going crazy if I thought that was going to work, but she really surprised me by saying that If I was serious

that she knew of a clairvoyant if that is what I really
wanted.

" You need to sort this out once and for all and clear
your mind so you can start to get on with your life",
she said.

I agreed and she said that she would contact me when
she had spoken to the person she knew. Two days
later after sleepless nights waiting and watching for
signs of paranormal activity, Katie phoned me and
said she had booked the woman for the following day
at 2.00 p.m.

Chapter 12

As promised the following day this lady who
looked more like a child arrived with Katie on the dot
at 2.00 p.m. She was quite small in stature about 4 foot

11 inches in height and when she introduced herself as Margo, her quiet, hushed voice matched her perfectly. "Let me explain what I am going to do", she said. "Clairvoyance is about connecting through visions, pictures and symbols. This requires intuitive guidance on my part and the skill and expertise to connect. Clairvoyance comes from the french clair- meaning clear, and voir - to see". "Visions may be symbolic and may symbolise the past or the present".

"First", she said, " we must choose a place where it is quiet and there will be no interruptions". "We will also need some soft background music to enable us to shut off unwanted chatter - mental or verbal". I informed her that with the soundproofing in the attic, it would be an ideal location with no interruption. We entered the attic and it was as if the very air stood still, as if it had been awaiting our arrival and now we were there, it was as if the atmosphere itself was afraid to breathe. Katie and I sat on the cushions I had placed there and Margo seemed quite happy to do the same. "Now", she said. "We must empty our minds of all that has happened to us today, we must open ourselves to the spirits so that they can enter here".

Margo took some deep breaths and seemed to be concentrating on something neither I nor Katie could see.

"I sense a presence". She said, and then was silent. "it feels like a small spirit, perhaps a child". Silence again. "Have you a message for someone here?" she asks.

The air in the room suddenly turned cold and the drums in the corner tapped twice and I'm sure that

Katie's heart must have nearly jumped out of her skin as I felt mine did. I was afraid to look at her and disturb the connection Margo seemed to have gained. "I'm sensing a little boy, he's pointing to the drums and himself so they must have belonged to him". "I feel such a strong sense of love here, this must have been such a happy home". Silence once more. "He's showing me a toy truck, but he's also a little sad". She laughs, "He's playing hide and seek with me, he wants to be found".

As she is saying this, I felt such a warm feeling all around me and just ever so slightly, a draught, as if a feather had flown by and touched me as it was passing. The hairs on my arms stood up as if I had been engulfed in static. I was afraid to look at Katie, afraid to break the connection that was now apparent.

Margo continued listening, "He's so tired now, he wants to go to sleep". The rocking chair in the corner starts rocking; very slowly and then gathering in momentum and then, suddenly, stops. "He is curling up on the floor, showing me darkness, there is no light where he is and the smell I am sensing is dank and musty. He is missing his family. He wants to come home.

Margo turned to us, "I feel that his spirit is stuck here, on the earth plain. He is perhaps lost, possibly because his earthly body is missing and needs to be found."

I sensed that Margo had finished although she appeared quite content to sit and listen to voices outside my hearing. She exuded a warmth as though there was a rosy aura surrounding her, a bright light, shining from within. I moved on the cushion and it seemed to break the spell. Margo looked up as if surprised as to where she was. I asked her if she was ok and she said yes it was time for her to go as she had another appointment. Katie and I accompanied Margo downstairs and I thanked her for her time. I asked Katie to stay and have coffee but she said she had to get back to the boys. I thanked her for finding Margo, gave her a hug and off she too went.

Chapter 13

I thought about the different options I had looked at and thought while the clairvoyant had been insightful, I still didn't have all the answers. So, I decided to use the ouija board to force the issue on my own. What did I have to lose right? I'd done the research. I know it's not a game but a sophisticated prediction tool that should only be used by someone who knows how to use it. I know it is recommended not to use it on your own but what the hell! I set it up in the attic as this was where there seemed to be the most activity and where the clairvoyant had connected with the child.

It was the middle of the night and everything was so still, so silent as if the whole world was in limbo. I needed silence and no distractions so that I could focus my undivided attention on the ouija board. I set the ambience by drawing a pentagram in which I would sit when I was ready and placing candles at each point of the pentagram. I set the ouija board up in the middle of the circle and thought about what I would ask. Should it be the old corny 'is there anybody there?' Hell I don't know.

I sat in the circle with the ouija board right in front of me hoping this would be a conduit to whatever was out there. I took deep breaths trying to calm myself in preparation for any unseen presence. I couldn't take notes as I needed both my hands to work the planchette. Deep breaths in, out, in, out, I felt a tremor in my fingertips as they touched the planchette. The planchette started moving and I concentrated on where it was going. My hands are trembling with fright or anticipation. I should have asked someone to do it with me. My fingers now are one with the planchette; I can't separate them or release them, but they are not making any sense, just a jumble of letters - no words. There seems to be whispers all around me emanating from the very walls. I became aware of tendrils of gossamer fibre surrounding me, light feathery strokes against my face and my body. Have I opened a dimensional portal? Am I finally going to get answers?

I sit still, listening, watching, waiting. All around me I can sense movement but I can't see anything. Suddenly I feel the slight touch of a child's hand on mine, not in any corporeal sense but manifesting itself lightly across my skin like walking through cobwebs, goosebumps pop up all over my arms, is this the one who has been calling me?

'What do you want?' I ask. Waiting for the planchette to move but instead a voice answers.

'Find me, please'.

'Tell me where you are and I will find you'.

'I'm here, I'm here, I'm here…

The voice tapers out and I'm left with an uneasy feeling. Fear is beginning to manifest itself as the movements around me coalesce into forms. Forms with no substance, just convergence of movement, darting around me, through me, in me. The drums in the corner start beating, not gently like before but throbbing to their own beat.; they won't stop. The rocking chair rocking to the beat of the drums, all the candles blew out, the attic light took on a life of its own. Swaying back and forth, back and forth constant, shadows evading the light as it trespassed into corners darkened by night.

I tried to push the planchette to goodbye. It's supposed to make it stop, but it just wouldn't do it - I tried and tried but it wouldn't let my fingers go, it was as if they were glued to the board as if there was a magnetic pole on the planchette. The wraiths just kept coming at me, more and more spectral apparitions dancing to the drumbeat, getting inside me, inside my mind, my body, god make them stop! These ghostly penetrations hurt the very centre of my core, what have I done!

Now

…Jean found me, huddled in the corner, so afraid. I collapsed into her arms, trembling, still unable to speak. Had I invoked something really bad? She helped me downstairs, soothing me as we descended the stairs and into the main room.

She sat me down on the sofa and continued to soothe me. I eventually found my voice and asked her what on earth had happened? I could hear her voice softly at first and then gain in strength as she tried to explain to me the events of the day and how she had come to find me. "I saw the light flashing through the skylight and wondered what was going on, so I came over to find you huddled in the corner", she said. "I think it's about time you found out the truth about this house". She continued to tell me the story she thought I might have discovered and left.

'3 years ago', she said 'a little boy disappeared from this house. On the day he disappeared, his mother had given him a row for leaving his toys on the stairs. She had nearly fallen over his truck which he had left at the bottom of the stairs and his toy cars which he had left on the curve at the bottom of the stairs. The parents searched everywhere for him but he was nowhere to be seen, they thought because he had had a row he was punishing them by hiding from them. He liked to play hide and seek. He also liked to sit on the third step on the stairs and play with his cars and would often be told off for leaving his truck there at the bottom of the stairs. The day the child went missing, the father had been working in the attic finishing putting in the panelling and soundproofing. It was going to be a place for them both to play drums and guitars, and, as they didn't want to disturb the neighbours, thought it would be a good idea. After telling her son off she went to carry on with dinner leaving the child on the stairs. Once finished she called her husband and her little boy. The husband came down but the child was nowhere to be seen. As soon as the mother realised her son was missing, she started screaming and crying his name. They searched everywhere for him, the house, the garden and fear of fears, the river.   But he was nowhere to be found. The police were called and they started combing the area for him and even called in volunteers to help look. The police questioned the mother and father but only the mother had seen him prior to going missing. The father said that he had been upstairs all day in the attic and had not seen him since that morning. There was no sight of him or evidence to connect him with anyone or anything. The mother said that she could hear him crying and calling for her. Three weeks later, unable to stay in the house, they left to stay with relatives.

The families that have lived here since have all said there were strange things happening, whispers, movement and strange sounds but no one there. I didn't tell you any of this because I wanted to have a friend that would stay. I've been watching you and waiting for something to happen hoping it wouldn't. 'So', I said. 'Is it the child that is haunting me?' 'Oh god, please tell me his name isn't Marc!

'How do you know that?', she asked.

I didn't move back into the house. I stayed with Jean. We talked and talked about what had occurred and I told her everything that had been going on and what I had done. I told her about the activity in the attic and she suggested it might be a good idea to go through the attic and we decided that we needed to find out what was exactly going on over there. So, the next day, Jean, Paul and I went over to the house and up to the attic armed with hammers and crowbars. We tore the attic apart, all the wood panelling and sound proofing in the Attic was going to come off. We each took a wall and started pulling everything off. I thought that I was going mad looking for something that probably wasn't there but needed to do this if only to convince myself it was real. And there it was. Using the crowbar I prised off the panelling to reveal a small door underneath the panelling tucked into a small crawl space, which would have opened out into the attic if it hadn't been covered over. I was shaking and scared to open the door. Scared of what I might find. I called Jean and Paul, and Paul told us to stand back while he opened the door. Waiting for that door to open has to be the worst moment of my life. Paul opened that door with the same trepidation on his face that we must have all been feeling, and there, lying on the floor, tucked into a foetal position was a small skeleton. I collapsed onto the floor and began sobbing.

Relief I wasn't going mad or pity for this poor little one that had been lost.

Chapter 14

Further investigation was to confirm that this was the child that had gone missing three years before. The police assumed he must have crawled into the space and fallen asleep as there was no evidence of foul play on the body. They came to the conclusion that the father must have closed the small door and panelled over it not having seen his son and without realising the child was in there. His cries would have not been heard because of the soundproofing installed under the panelling.

Only his mother heard the sounds.

His haunting of me, was a cry for help.

Printed in Great Britain
by Amazon

43650637R00056